by Rich Tommaso

A **tea leaves** CAPER

FLOATING WORLD COMICS

OTHER COMIC BOOKS BY RICH TOMMASO

CLOVER HONEY
LET'S HIT THE ROAD
THE HORROR OF COLLIER COUNTY
8 1/2 GHOSTS
PERVERSO!
PETE AND MIRIAM
THE CAVALIER MR. THOMPSON
DRY COUNTY
DARK CORRIDOR
SHE WOLF
SPY SEAL : THE CORTEN-STEEL PHOENIX
THE MYSTERIOUS CASE

FLOATING WORLD COMICS PRESENTS
IN THE GARDEN OF EARTHLY DELIGHTS
A TEA LEAVES CAPER

IN THE GARDEN OF EARTHLY DELIGHTS by Rich Tommaso © Published by Floating World Comics 2024. Originally published by BP Communications, Inc. All rights reserved. Nothing may be printed in whole or in part without written permission from the publisher and artists. Any similarity to real people and places in fiction and semifiction is purely coincidental.

PART ONE
SOMEBODY OWES ME A MILLION DOLLARS

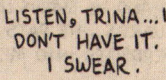

"LISTEN, TRINA...I DON'T HAVE IT. I SWEAR."

"NO KIDDING...HERE WE GO, DINA...OKAY, HULOT--I'M PUTTING THE WORD OUT THERE THAT YOU STIFFED US AND THAT NO ONE SHOULD USE YOU AS A FENCE ANYMORE..."

"NO! DON'T DO THAT! LISTEN TO ME..."

 "I DON'T HAVE TO TELL YOU THOSE JEWELS WERE SOME HOT ITEMS! OTHERWISE, I COULD'VE SOLD 'EM TO A DOZEN GUYS! BUT **NOBODY** WANTED TO TOUCH THEM..."

THEN A FRIEND RECOMMENDS A BUYER...ETIENNE MANCHETTE. AN ART & JEWELRY COLLECTOR. AND... AN **ARMS DEALER**!

A RISK-TAKER, HE ASSURES ME...AND FILTHY RICH, SO WE'D HAVE NO TROUBLE GETTING THE CASH...

Ⓑ WE BURY THE ART AND LAY LOW--LET ALL THE NEWSPAPERS DO THEIR THING... 	Ⓒ WE SEND WORD OUT TO THE UNDERWORLD THAT A GROUP OF CANADIAN **MEN** DID THE HEIST-- AND NEED A BUYER... 
Ⓓ WE WAIT 'TIL ETIENNE BITES--WE ALL **KNOW** THAT HE WILL...	Ⓔ WE'LL NEED MASKED MEN TO MAKE THE SALE. **ARMED** TOO! "EASY!" 
Ⓕ THEY'LL SHOW HIM **ONE** OF THE PIECES, AN EXCELLENT FAKE... 	Ⓖ BUT, THEY'LL **ALL** BE FAKES! WE TAKE HIM FOR MILLIONS AND **HE** GETS BURNED! "SORRY." 

EXTRA! LA TIMES EXTRA!
BIGGEST ART HEIST EVER!

PART TWO
THIS IS NOT A PICASSO

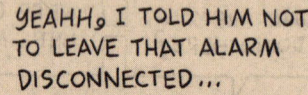

7 IN THE COMING DAYS, WORD GETS AROUND ABOUT THE HEIST--PULLED OFF BY A GROUP OF "CANADIANS".

PART THREE

IN THE GARDEN OF EVIL

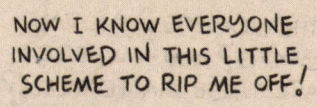

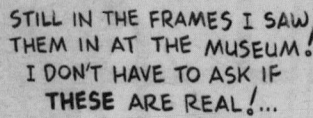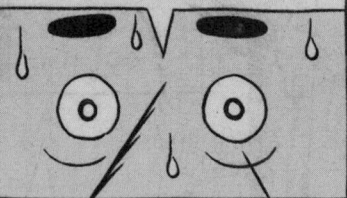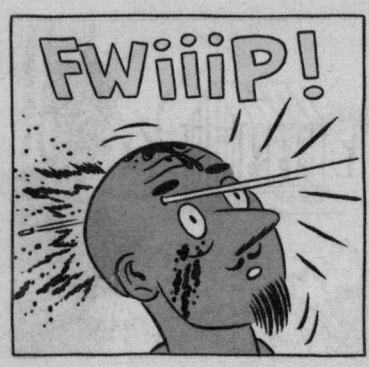

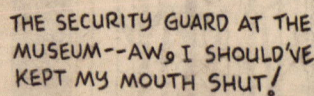

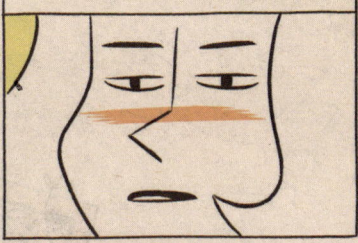